Written by **Nancy Parent**
Illustrated by **Luigi Aimè, Tomatofarm**

Thomas the Tank Engine & Friends™

CREATED BY BRITT ALLCROFT

Based on the Railway Series by the Reverend W Awdry
© 2018 Gullane (Thomas) LLC.
Thomas the Tank Engine & Friends and Thomas & Friends are trademarks of Gullane (Thomas) LLC. Thomas the Tank Engine & Friends and Design Is Reg. U.S. Pat. & Tm. Off.
© 2018 HIT Entertainment Limited. HIT and the HIT logo are trademarks of HIT Entertainment Limited. All rights reserved.
Published in the United States by Random House Children's Books, a division of Penguin Random House LLC, 1745 Broadway, New York, NY 10019,
and in Canada by Penguin Random House Canada Limited, Toronto. Random House and the colophon are registered trademarks of Penguin Random House LLC.
Visit us on the Web!
rhcbooks.com   www.thomasandfriends.com
ISBN 978-1-5247-6731-0
MANUFACTURED IN CHINA
10 9 8 7 6 5 4 3 2 1
Random House Children's Books supports the First Amendment and celebrates the right to read.

HiT entertainment

TAKE YOUR TURN!

Random House New York

It was a lovely day on the Island of Sodor. Sir Topham Hatt went to the Search and Rescue Center to talk to Flynn and Belle.

"I want you to take turns practicing your fire drills today," he told them.

Then he headed for Tidmouth Sheds to find Thomas.

"Thomas," Sir Topham Hatt began, "please go to the Search and Rescue Center to help Flynn and Belle with their drills."

"Yes, Sir," Thomas puffed happily. He felt glad to be doing something Really Useful.

Soon Thomas chuffed up to the
Search and Rescue Center.
"Sir Topham Hatt wants to make
sure you and Belle are ready for any
emergency," he explained to Flynn.
"I'm here to help you with your drills."

"That's great news, Thomas!" Flynn said. "Belle and I are ready and rarin' to go! Aren't we, Belle?"

But before Belle could say a word, Flynn got busy testing his rail wheels on the track.

Next, Flynn tested his four road wheels.
"Way to drive, Flynn!" Thomas puffed.

"Do you want to show me your firefighting equipment?" Thomas asked both engines.

"Absolutely," Flynn replied as he quickly unwound and rewound his long fire hoses.

Belle was about to ring her bell for Thomas when Flynn pulled out his long ladder.

"Look, Thomas!" he called, raising the ladder toward the sky.

Belle watched
without a word.

Soon it was time to fill up at the water tower. Flynn and Belle needed to test their water cannons. Flynn went first—and used up most of the water.

By the time Belle got her turn, there was only a trickle left.

Thomas asked Harold to help with the next drill.

"If your water reaches all the way to Harold," said Thomas, "it will show that your cannons are strong enough to fight faraway fires."

"I'll go first," Flynn said.

"You're next, Belle," said Thomas.

But when Belle aimed her water cannons, only a tiny stream flowed out.

"Oh, dear," she said. "I don't have enough water. I've failed the test."

Flynn and Thomas saw that Belle was upset.
"This is my fault," said Flynn. "I didn't give Belle
enough of a turn at the water tower. I also didn't give
her a turn to test her equipment."
Flynn apologized to his friend. "I'm sorry, Belle. I guess
I was too impatient. I wanted to start practicing."

There was enough time for the engines to do another fire drill.
They took turns filling up at a different water tower.

This time, Flynn let Belle go first.

Then Belle and Flynn
puffed over to the
water's edge for their
final fire drill.

They each took turns aiming at the buoys next to Captain.

"Looks like all water cannons are working!" Thomas said.

"I think you'll both be ready if a real fire breaks out," said Captain with a big smile.

The last things that needed checking
were the horns, bells, and whistles.
Flynn let Belle go first.
"Peep, peep!" she whistled happily.

When Sir Topham Hatt returned, he was very pleased. "Well done, you two," he said, smiling at Belle and Flynn. "Thomas told me that by taking turns during your drills, both of you showed that you're prepared for emergencies. You are two Really Useful Fire Engines!"

Learning to Be a Good Friend

Dear Parents and Caregivers,

Welcome to the world of Thomas & Friends™! This storybook series, focused on helping toddlers and preschoolers build friendship skills, is designed to engage, enrich, and delight you and your child. You will see how Thomas and his friends work together to solve problems and how they build relationships along the way.

Storybooks in the series will include such themes as sharing, taking turns, teamwork, feelings, respecting rules, making friends, and fear of the dark. In these stories, children will see how the characters behave, react, suffer consequences, and solve problems in different situations. This can encourage conversations about social and emotional skills and participation in cooperative play, help with understanding and expressing feelings, and promote behaviors such as comforting a playmate, resolving disagreements, engaging in teamwork, following rules, and respecting others.

There's nothing Thomas and his friends like better than to be "Really Useful." In this series, these charming characters model and reinforce the behaviors involved in forming first friendships. At the end of each story, you'll find a sample discussion and suggested questions to support the message. For young fans of Thomas, he may prove to be the most *Useful* friend of all!

Dr. Deborah Weber, PhD
Director, Early Childhood Development Research
Fisher-Price

Developing positive relationship skills enables children to interact in socially appropriate ways to achieve common goals. Taking turns is a collaboration skill that gives children a chance to play with a shared object or to take part in an activity involving others. This interaction encourages playing together and forming successful relationships.

Shared Reading

Research consistently links the frequency of shared book reading to a preschool child's emergent literacy skills and also later reading comprehension. The example below demonstrates shared reading dialogue between a reader and a child.

Adult: How do you think Belle felt when Flynn used up most of the water on his turn?

Child: Sad, because there wasn't any water left for her.

Adult: You're right—she felt sad. What do you think Flynn should have done?

Child: Stopped filling up with water after just a few minutes so Belle could have her turn.

Adult: Yes, Flynn should have let Belle have a turn so she didn't feel sad. Friends should take turns so everyone gets a chance and no one feels sad.

Suggested Questions

Use the following questions to talk with children about friendship and taking turns.

- What was Thomas going to help Flynn and Belle do?
- Can you think of a time when you helped a friend?
- Why didn't Flynn take turns with Belle?
- What made Flynn realize Belle hadn't had a fair turn at the water tower?
- How did Flynn feel when he realized he hadn't given Belle a real turn?
- How do you think Belle felt when Flynn apologized to her?
- What happened after the engines took turns filling up at the second water tower?
- What did Thomas tell Sir Topham Hatt at the end of the story?
- Why is it important to take turns when you're playing with friends?
- How does it make you feel when a friend doesn't let you have a turn?

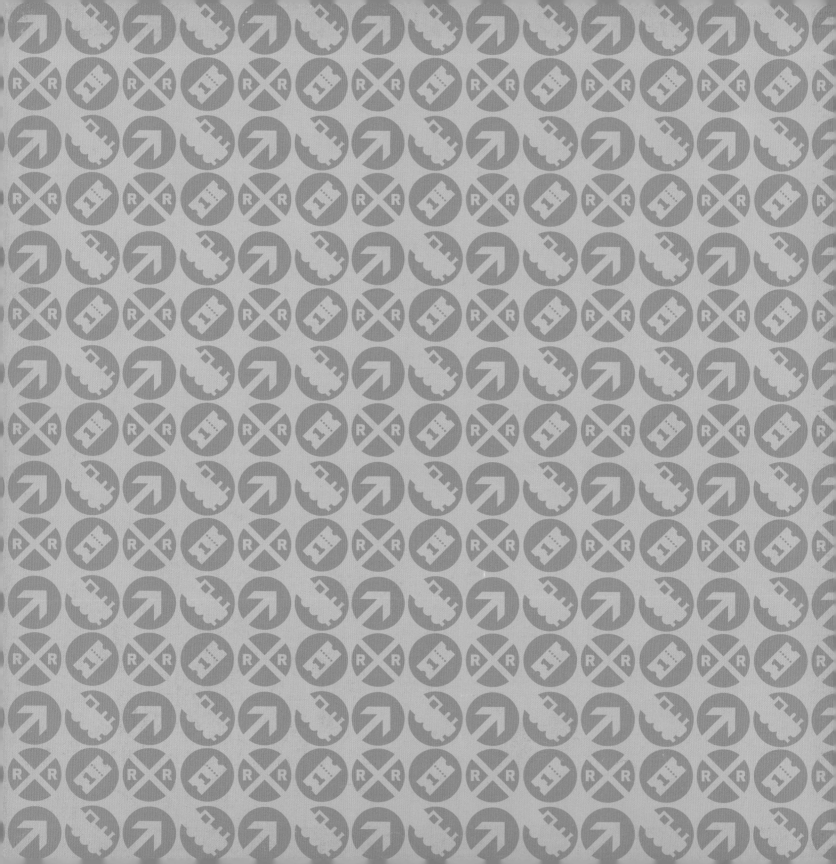